The LIVING SEA

Adaptation from the animated series: Robin Bright
Illustrations: Guru Animation Studio Ltd.

CRACKBOOM!

It's so hot today! True and Bartleby are with the Rainbow King cooling off at the beach. True is getting thirsty.

But someone has drunk all the zazoony juice balls! Who could it be?

SLURRRP! It's a Sea Blubb on the other side of a sand dune. "So it was you!" says True. "Should we go for a swim to cool off?"
The Sea Blubb crawls under a palm tree. "A Sea Blubb that doesn't want to go in the sea? That's not Sea Blubby at all!"

True dips her finger into the water. "The water is really warm. Too warm for the Sea Blubbs. Maybe something's wrong with the Living Sea!"

"The best way to find out," the Rainbow King says, "is to ask her."

True is amazed. "You know the Living Sea?"

"Oh, yes! We go way back," the Rainbow King replies. "I knew her when she was just a puddle. Let's go!"

"Oh, wide and wonderful Living Sea," the Rainbow King declares from his castle, "I ask that you please meet with me!"
A wave rises high into the air and the Living Sea appears, in all her majesty!

But she tells a sad story: "The ice stars that have always kept me cool have mysteriously disappeared. Now I am too warm for the Sea Blubbs."

True and Bartleby go searching for the missing ice stars with Cumulo, but can't find any! "We need some Wish help," says True. "To the Wishing Tree!"

"Zee, the Living Sea is too warm for the Sea Blubbs," says True at the Wishing Tree. "The ice stars that keep the water cool are missing."

"That is serious," says Zee. "Let's sit and have a think about this."

The three friends sit down on the mushrooms. They each take a deep breath.

True says, "I need a Wish that can help me search underwater for the ice stars. Then I need another Wish to cool down the Living Sea right away."

"The Wishing Tree has heard you, True," replies Zee.

"It's time to get your three Wishes."

WISHING TREE,
WISHING TREE,
PLEASE SHARE YOUR WONDERFUL
WISHES WITH ME.

The Wishes wake up and spin around True.
Three Wishes stay with her, and the others return
to the Wishing Tree.

"Very interesting Wishes," Zee says. "I can tell you more about their powers. Let's check the Wishopedia."

CHILLZY
freezes things instantly.

WHOMPIT
loves to whomp and stomp.

BUBBA
helps you breathe underwater.

"Thank you, Zee. And thank you, Wishing Tree, for sharing your Wishes with me," True says, as she leaves with the Wishes in her pack.

When she gets back to the Living Sea, True discovers that another ice star has vanished. She must hurry! True activates her first Wish.

"I choose you. Wake up, Chillzy! Wish come true!"

Chillzy freezes as much of the water as he can, but the surface of the Living Sea is too big and won't stay cool for long.

To help her search for the ice stars, True activates her second Wish. "Zip, Zap, Zoo! I choose you, Bubba! Wish come true!" Now she can breathe underwater! She finds the last ice star— but someone has tied a rope around it! Who's taking it away?

True returns to the surface and hops onto Cumulo's back with
Bartleby. Together, they follow the ice star.

They touch down in a little cove. Bartleby dips his paw in the
water: It's freezing cold. They must be getting closer to the ice stars!

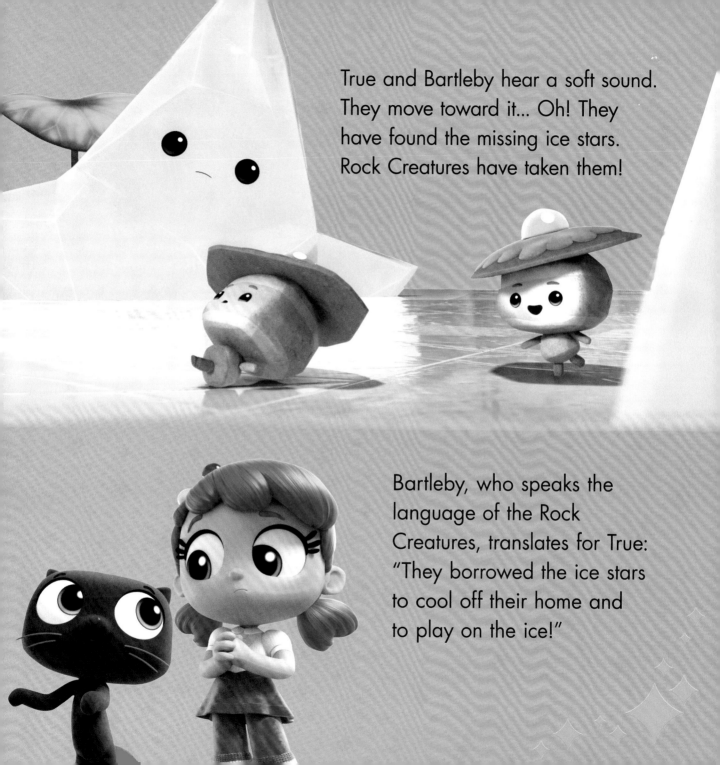

True and Bartleby hear a soft sound.
They move toward it... Oh! They
have found the missing ice stars.
Rock Creatures have taken them!

Bartleby, who speaks the
language of the Rock
Creatures, translates for True:
"They borrowed the ice stars
to cool off their home and
to play on the ice!"

"But the ice stars belong in the Living Sea," True replies. "Without them, her water is too warm for the Sea Blubbs."

The Rock Creatures are so sorry. They didn't know! They'll return the ice stars to the Living Sea right away.

With the help of the Rock Creatures, True and Bartleby try to move the ice stars. And try. And try.
But the ice stars won't budge. They are frozen in place!

True has an idea. She activates her last Wish.

ZIP ZAP ZOO!

"I choose you! Wake up, Whompit! Wish come true!"

By whomping and stomping, Whompit is able to break up all of the ice.

The powerful Wish sets the ice stars free! The Rock Creatures can bring them back home to the Living Sea.

The Sea Blubbs can feel the difference right away! The Rainbow King spots one playing in the waves. "Is the temperature of the water to your liking?" he asks.

The Sea Blubb barks happily. "All nice and cool again!" says True.

The Rock Creatures promise not to take anything out of the Living Sea from now on. They'll be back in the winter for more ice skating, but they might return sooner. "Because they've made new friends!" laughs True. "Us!"

CrackBoom! Books is an imprint of Chouette Publishing (1987) Inc.

Text: adaptation by Robin Bright of the animated series TRUE AND THE RAINBOW KINGDOM™/MC,
produced by Guru Studio.
Original script written by John Slama
Original episode #113: The Living Sea
All rights reserved.
Illustrations: ©GURU STUDIO. All Rights Reserved.

Chouette Publishing would like to thank the Government of Canada and SODEC
for their financial support.

Canada

Québec
Books
Tax Credit
Gestion
SODEC

Bibliothèque et Archives nationales du Québec and Library and Archives
Canada cataloguing in publication

Title: The living sea/adaptation, Robin Bright; illustration, Guru Animation Studio.
Names: Bright, Robin, 1966- author. | Guru Studio (Firm), illustrator
Description: Series statement: True and the rainbow kingdom
Identifiers: Canadiana 20200071254 | ISBN 9782898022234 (softcover)
Classification: LCC PZ7.1.B75 Li 2020 | DDC j813/.6—dc23

Legal deposit – Bibliothèque et Archives nationales du Québec, 2020.
Legal deposit – Library and Archives Canada, 2020.

Printed in Canada
10 9 8 7 6 5 4 3 2 1   CHO2094 MAY2020